Stories for 6 Year Olds

This is a Dempsey Parr Book
First published in 2000

Dempsey Parr is an imprint of Parragon
Parragon
Queen Street House, 4 Queen Street,
Bath, BA1 1HE, UK

Produced by The Templar Company plc
Pippbrook Mill, London Road, Dorking,
Surrey, RH4 1JE, UK

Printed and bound in Spain
ISBN 1 84084 826 X

Stories for 6 Year Olds

DP
DEMPSEY
PARR

Contents

London Bridge is Falling Down

London bridge is falling down,
Falling down, falling down,
London bridge is falling down,
My fair lady.

Build it up with wood and clay,
Wood and clay, wood and clay,
Build it up with wood and clay,
My fair lady

Wood and clay will wash away,
Wash away, wash away,
Wood and clay will wash away,
My fair lady.

Build it up with bricks and mortar,
Bricks and mortar, bricks and mortar,
Build it up with bricks and mortar,
My fair lady.

Bricks and mortar will not stay,
Will not stay, will not stay,
Bricks and mortar will not stay,
My fair lady.

Build it up with iron and steel,
Iron and steel, iron and steel,
Build it up with iron and steel,
My fair lady.

Iron and steel will bend and bow,
Bend and bow, bend and bow
Iron and steel will bend and bow,
My fair lady.

Build it up with silver and gold,
Silver and gold, silver and gold,
Build it up with silver and gold,
My fair lady.

Silver and gold will be stolen away,
Stolen away, stolen away,
Silver and gold will be stolen away,
My fair lady.

Set a man to watch all night,
Watch all night, watch all night,
Set a man to watch all night,
My fair lady.

Ursula's Umbrella

Ursula was a little girl who longed for adventure. She loved reading stories about far-away places and explorers, and even children like herself who had amazing adventures. "Why doesn't anything interesting ever happen to me?" she sighed. "How I wish I could fly to the moon or dive to the deepest part of the ocean. What fun it would be!"

One windy day, Ursula went out for a walk. She took her umbrella with her because it looked as though it might be going to rain. Ursula's umbrella was red with a shiny black handle. It was also very large indeed. People used to laugh as Ursula walked along the street with her umbrella up. It looked so big and Ursula was so small that it seemed as though the umbrella was walking along all by itself!

As Ursula walked up the street she felt a few raindrops on her nose. "Better put up my umbrella," she thought. She unfurled her umbrella and lifted it up above her head. As she did so, a great gust of wind came and swept her right off the pavement. It carried her past the upstairs windows of the houses, past the roofs and the chimney pots and up, up, into the sky. Ursula clung tightly to the umbrella handle. She was surprised to find she didn't feel the least bit frightened. No, not a bit. She felt very excited. She looked down and saw streets and houses whizzing past far below. Then she saw fields and something that looked like a silver thread snaking through the countryside. "A river!" thought Ursula.

Now she could see the coastline, and soon the umbrella was carrying her out over the ocean. At first when she looked down the sea was gray, but gradually it turned to the deepest blue with frothy white waves. "How I'd love a swim," thought Ursula. At that moment she felt the umbrella starting to descend. Looking down she could see that they were heading for an island in the middle of the ocean. Soon she was floating past the tops of palm trees and, as she touched the ground, she felt sand under her feet.

"I'm going for a swim!" said Ursula to herself. She folded up her umbrella and set off to the beach. The water felt deliciously warm as Ursula paddled about. She looked down and saw that the water was amazingly clear. She could see brightly colored fish darting in and out of the coral. "Wow!" exclaimed Ursula out loud and then "Wow!" again, though this time much louder as she looked up and saw a black fin skimming through the water towards her. "Shark!" she shrieked, but no-one heard.

Then all of a sudden a gust of wind made her umbrella unfurl itself and float towards her in the water, like a boat. Ursula made a dash for the umbrella, hurled herself into it and floated away across the sea. "That was quite an adventure!" she thought.

After a while, Ursula looked out over the rim of the umbrella and saw that it was heading for the shore again. This time, when Ursula stepped out of the umbrella, she found that she was at the edge of a jungle. Folding up the umbrella, she set off into the forest. She followed an overgrown path through the trees. "I wonder where this leads?" thought Ursula. She wiped her brow and swatted the insects that flew in front of her face. Deeper and deeper into the jungle she went.

Suddenly she heard the sound of rushing water and found herself standing on the banks of a river. All at once she heard another sound. It was the crashing noise of some enormous beast approaching through the trees.

Where could she run to? Suddenly she felt the umbrella being blown from her hand. To her amazement it fell to the ground, stretching right across the river like a bridge. Ursula walked over to the other side, not daring to look down at the torrent below. When she was safely on the far bank she looked back to see a large puma, with glittering green eyes, glaring at her from the opposite bank. "That was a lucky escape!" thought Ursula.

Ursula could see a mountain through the trees and decided to head towards it. "I'll be able to get a good view from the top and maybe find my way home," she thought. She struggled on through the forest and eventually found herself at the foot of the mountain. There seemed to be no way up the sheer rock face.

Ursula was on the point of despair when suddenly another great gust of wind blew up. It carried Ursula, clinging to her opened umbrella, all the way up to the top of the mountain.

At the top of the mountain, the umbrella let her gently down again and her feet landed in deep snow. By now it was blowing a blizzard and she could not see anything except white snowflakes in all directions. "There's only one thing to do," thought Ursula. She put the umbrella on the snow, sat on it and whizzed all the way down the other side of the mountain.

When she reached the bottom, to her surprise, the umbrella sled didn't stop but carried on through the snowstorm until eventually, after a very long time, it came to a halt right outside her own front door. "Well, that was quite an adventure," said Ursula, shaking the snow off the umbrella, before folding it up.

She stepped inside the front door. "Wherever have you been?" said her mother. "You look as though you've been to the ends of the Earth and back."

"Well I have," Ursula was about to say. But then she thought that no-one would believe her and it was nicer to keep her adventures to herself. And that is what she did.

Peter Meets a Dragon

Once upon a time there was a young boy named Peter. He lived in an ordinary house with an ordinary mum and dad, an ordinary sister and an ordinary pet cat, called Jasper. In fact, everything in Peter's life was so ordinary that he sometimes wished that something extraordinary would happen. "Why doesn't a giant come and squash the house flat with his foot?" he wondered, and "If only a pirate would take my sister hostage!" But each day, Peter would wake up in the morning and everything was just the same as it had been the day before.

One morning Peter woke up to find a very strange smell in the house. Looking out of his bedroom window, he saw that the front lawn was scorched and blackened. There was smoke drifting off the grass and, further away, he could see some bushes ablaze.

Peter rushed downstairs and out of the front door. He ran out of the yard and down the street following the trail of smoke and burning grass. He grew more and more puzzled, however, as there was no sign of anything that could have caused such a blaze.

Peter was about to run home and tell his mum and dad, when he heard a panting noise coming from the undergrowth. Parting the bushes gently with his hands he found a young creature. It had green, scaly skin, a pair of wings and a long snout full of sharp teeth. Every now and again a little tongue of flame came from its nostrils, setting the grass around it on fire. "A baby dragon!" Peter said to himself, in great surprise. Big tears were rolling out of the dragon's yellow eyes and down its scaly cheeks as it flapped its wings desperately and tried to take off.

When the dragon saw Peter it stopped flapping its wings. "Oh, woe is me!" it sobbed. "Where am I?"

"Where do you want to be?" asked Peter, kneeling down on the scorched ground.

"I want to be in Dragonland with my friends," replied the dragon. "We were all flying together, but I just couldn't keep up with them. I got tired and needed a rest. I called to the others but they didn't hear me. Then I just had to stop and get my breath back. Now I don't know where I am, or if I'll ever see my friends again!" And with that the baby dragon started to cry once more.

"I'm sure I can help. I'll get you home," said Peter, though he had no idea how.

"You?" hissed a voice nearby. "How could you possibly help? You're just a boy!" Peter looked round, and to his astonishment found Jasper sitting behind him. "I suppose you're going to wave a magic wand, are you?" continued Jasper. "You need to call in an expert." Then he turned his back on Peter and the baby dragon and started washing his paws.

Peter was astounded. He'd never heard Jasper talking before. He had thought he was just an ordinary pet cat. "W… w… what do you mean?" he stammered.

"Well," said Jasper, glancing over his shoulder at Peter, "I reckon that horse over there could help. Follow me."

So Peter and the baby dragon – whose name was Flame – followed Jasper over to where the horse stood at the edge of a field. Jasper leaped up on to the gate and called to the horse. Then he whispered in the horse's ear. The horse thought for a moment, then whispered back in Jasper's ear. "He says he's got a friend on the other side of the wood who'll help," said Jasper.

"But how?" asked Peter, looking perplexed.

"Be patient! Follow me!" said Jasper as he stalked off through the grass. "And tell your friend to stop setting fire to everything!" he added. Peter saw, to his horror, that Flame was indeed blazing a trail through the field.

"I can't help it," cried Flame, about to burst into tears again. "Every time I get out of breath I start to pant, and then I start breathing fire."

"Let me carry you," said Peter. He picked Flame up in his arms and ran after Jasper. The baby dragon felt very strange. His body was all cold and clammy, but his mouth was still breathing hot smoke, which made Peter's eyes water.

He ran through the wood, just keeping Jasper's upright tail in sight. On the other side of the wood was another field, and in the field was a horse. But this was no ordinary horse. Peter stopped dead in his tracks and stared. The horse was pure milky white, and from its head grew a single, long horn. "A unicorn!" breathed Peter.

Jasper was already talking to the unicorn. He beckoned with his paw to Peter. "He'll take your friend home and you can go, too, Peter, but don't be late for supper, or you know what your mother will say." And with that, Jasper was off.

"Climb aboard," said the unicorn gently.

Peter and the little dragon scrambled up on to the unicorn's back. "What an adventure," thought Peter. Up, up, and away they soared through the clouds.

Flame held tightly on to Peter's hand with his clammy paw. At last Peter could see a mountain ahead through the clouds. Now they were descending through the clouds again, and soon the unicorn landed right at the top of the mountain. "I'm home!" squeaked Flame happily as they landed. Sure enough,

several dragons were running over to greet him. They looked quite friendly, but some of them were rather large and one was breathing a great deal of fire.

"Time for me to go," said Peter a little nervously, as Flame jumped off the unicorn's back and flew to the ground. The unicorn took off again and soon they were back in the field once more.

As he slid off the unicorn's back, Peter turned to thank him, but when he looked he saw that it was just an ordinary horse with no trace of a horn at all. Peter walked back home across the field, but there was no sign of burnt grass. He reached his own front lawn, which was also in perfect condition. Peter felt more and more perplexed. "I hope Jasper can explain," he thought, as the cat ran past him and into the house. "Jasper, I took the baby dragon home. What's happened to the burnt grass?" he blurted out. But Jasper said not a word. He ignored Peter and curled up in his basket.

When Peter wasn't looking, however, Jasper gave him a glance that seemed to say, "Well, was that a big enough adventure for you?"

GEE UP, TEDDY

Gee up, Teddy,
Don't you stop!
Ride on the
hobbyhorse,
Clippety clop!
Clippety clopping,
Round and round.
Giddy up,
We're toybox bound!

THREE TEDS IN A TUB

Rub-a-dub, dub,
Three teds in a tub,
Sailing across the sea!
But the rumble of tums,
And the smell of hot buns,
Will bring them back home for tea!

MIDNIGHT FUN

Just as midnight's striking,
When everyone's asleep,
Teddies yawn and stretch and shake,
And out of warm beds creep.

They sneak out from their houses,
And gather in the dark,
Then skip along the empty streets,
Heading for the park.

And there beneath the moonlight,
They tumble down the slides,
They swoosh up high upon the swings,
And play on all the rides.

And when the sun comes peeping,
They rush home to their beds,
And snuggle down as children wake,
To cuddle with their teds!

MESSAGE IN A BOTTLE

Frosty, the polar bear, dipped a huge hairy paw into a hole in the ice and felt about. He was sure he had seen something glimmering beneath the surface of the water. Just then, Beaky, the penguin, popped up through the hole, clutching something under his wing. It was a glass bottle.

"I thought I saw something odd," said Frosty. "What is it?"

"I don't know," said Beaky. "I found it in the sea, far away on the other side of the icebergs. It was floating on the waves."

The two friends sat and looked at the bottle.

"There's something inside," said Beaky. "Let's take it out." They took out the cork and Beaky reached inside with his beak and pulled out a note.

"What does it say?" asked Frosty.

Beaky peered closely at the note.

"It says: 'Help. I am stranded on a desert island. My boat is broken. It is very hot. Love Browny, the bear,'" read Beaky. "There's a map on the other side. Do you think we should help?"

"Of course we should," said Frosty. "It sounds like one of my cousins is in trouble. Anyway, it will be a great adventure! I've always wanted to know what hot feels like!"

The two friends studied the map carefully, then set off across the ice and snow until they reached the sea. They turned and waved goodbye to their chilly home, dove into the icy water and started to swim south in the direction of the desert island. After a while, Frosty began to feel tired. He had never swum so far away from home before.

"Let's rest a moment," said Beaky, and they flipped over in the water and lay floating along on their backs.

"Do you think it's much further?" asked Frosty.

"Oh, yes, much further," said Beaky. "The water has not even begun to get warm yet. By the time we get there it will be like taking a hot bath."

"I've never had one of those!" said Frosty, excitedly. "Will I like it?"

"I'm not sure," said Beaky.

So the two friends carried on swimming towards the sunshine. Gradually the water grew warmer and warmer. Frosty started to laugh.

"My skin's all nice and tingly," he chuckled.

On and on they swam. The bright sun beat down on their heads. By now Frosty was puffing and panting with every stroke.

"I think I must be feeling hot," he said. "I don't think I can swim much further!

"You don't have to!" said Beaky, pointing with his wing. "There's the island!"

On the shore, Browny was jumping up and down with excitement and waving his paws.

"You found me!" he cried. "Imagine my little bottle floating all the way to the North Pole!"

"Imagine me swimming all the way here from the North Pole!" panted Frosty, as he staggered out of the sea and collapsed in a heap on the hot sand. "I'm exhausted!"

Browny led his rescuers to the shelter of a cave he had found nearby, and they rested there until they recovered. As night fell, Browny built a fire on the beach, and they sat telling stories. He told them all about finding a little boat and setting sail across the sea, and how his boat had been shipwrecked.

"I thought I would be stranded here for ever!" Browny said. "And I want to go home!"

"Don't worry," said Frosty. "We'll get you home. But first let's get a good night's rest."

The next morning the three friends had great fun playing on the beach.

"I'm not sure I like hot, though," said Frosty, "it makes me tired and uncomfortable. And this sand stuff gets everywhere!" The others laughed.

"Let's be on our way then," said Beaky.

And so they set back off across the ocean, pulling Browny along on a raft he'd made, as he wasn't a good swimmer like the others. It was another long, hard journey, but when they finally reached Browny's home and saw how happy he was to be back there, they knew it was worth it.

"Promise you'll come and visit me again!" cried Browny, as the others waved goodbye and set off once more for their chilly home.

"We will!" cried Frosty. "But not if you're somewhere hot. I can't wait to get home for a good slide on the ice!"

THE BEAR WILL HAVE TO GO

While Lucy slept in the shade of a tree, Cuthbert went for a walk into the woods and was soon quite lost. He had no idea which way was back, so he sat down and thought about what to do next.

When Lucy awoke, she looked around in surprise. Her teddy bear, Cuthbert, was missing. She thought someone had taken him, for she didn't know that when people are asleep their teddy bears like to go walking.

"Cuthbert!" she called. "Cuthbert, where are you?"

He wasn't very far away. Lucy soon found him sniffing at a clump of moss.

"There you are!" she sighed. "I thought I'd lost you. Where's your waistcoat?"

In fact, Lucy really had lost Cuthbert, for the bear she was now taking home was not a teddy bear at all, but a real baby bear cub! As they ran back through the woods, the bear in Lucy's arms kept very still. He stared straight ahead without blinking, and tried not to sneeze. Soon they were back in Lucy's bedroom. Lucy flung the bear on her bed, then went to run a bath.

"Time to escape!" thought the bear. He slid off the bed, pulling the covers after him. He ran over to the window and tried to climb up the curtains. They tore down and tumbled to a heap on the floor. Just then Lucy's mother came into the room. The bear froze. Then Lucy appeared.

"Look at this mess," said Lucy's mother. "You've been playing with that bear again. Please tidy up."

Lucy had no idea how her room had got in such a mess, but she tidied up, took the bear into the bathroom and put him on the edge of the tub.

"Don't fall in," she said, and went to fetch a towel. The bear jumped into the tub with a great splash. He waved his paws wildly sending sprays of soapy water across the room. When he heard footsteps, he froze and floated on his back in the water as if nothing was wrong. It was Lucy, followed by her mother. "Oh, Lucy! What a mess!"

"Cuthbert must have fallen in," cried Lucy, rubbing his wet fur with a towel.

"A teddy bear couldn't make all this mess on its own," said Lucy's mother. "Please clean it up."

Lucy looked carefully at Cuthbert. Something was different about him, but she just couldn't work out what it was.

That night, while Lucy slept, the bear tip-toed downstairs. He needed to get back to the woods where he belonged, but he was hungry. In the kitchen he found lots of food, and he had a feast.

When Lucy came down for a glass of milk she found him with food all over his paws. The bear froze. Then her mother appeared in the doorway.

"This is the last straw, Lucy," said her mother, crossly. "You have been very naughty today, and every time something happens you've got that bear with you. If there is any more bad behaviour, the bear will have to go."

When her mother had gone back upstairs, Lucy looked carefully at the bear.

"You're not Cuthbert are you?" she said. The bear looked back at her and blinked. Lucy gasped. "You're a real bear!"

Now all the mess made sense! Lucy could hardly believe she had made such a mistake. She stroked the bear gently and he licked her finger.

"I'd better get you back to the woods before there's any more trouble," she said. "And I'd better try to find the real Cuthbert."

So early next morning, before her parents were awake, she crept out of the house carrying the bear. Out in the woods she put the bear on the ground. He licked her hand and padded away.

Lucy was sad to see the little bear go. She wiped a tear from her eye as she turned away... and there at the foot of a tree sat her teddy bear, Cuthbert! Lucy picked him up and hugged him.

"Where have you been?" she asked. "You'll never guess the trouble I've been in. What have you been doing all night?"

Cuthbert said nothing. He just smiled. What had he been doing all night? Well, that's another story!

Rapunzel

There once lived a man and his wife who had long wished for a child. At last their wish was granted and the wife found that she was expecting a baby. At the back of their house was a garden that was filled with the most beautiful flowers and herbs. However, the man and his wife did not dare enter the garden, for it was owned by a wicked witch, of whom everyone was scared.

One day, when the woman was standing by her window looking down into the garden, she saw a flower bed full of the prettiest Rapunzel plants she had ever seen. They looked so fresh and green that she felt a great craving to eat some of them. Day after day she would sit by her window, staring at the Rapunzel plants for hours on end. Eventually she became quite pale and miserable.

"What's wrong, my dear?" said her husband.

"I must have some of that Rapunzel," she replied, "or I may die."

The poor husband decided that the only thing to do was to steal into the witch's garden at night and take some of the plants. Late one night the man climbed the high wall that surrounded the garden and hastily snatched a bunch of Rapunzel plants and made off with them.

His wife was delighted. She made a salad of them that was so delicious that the next day she said to her husband, "I must have more of that delicious Rapunzel."

So that night the husband stole once more into the witch's garden. Imagine his horror when he dropped on to the grass to find the witch there lying in wait for him. "How dare you come into my garden and steal my Rapunzel plants," she shrieked. "You'll live to regret this."

"Please have mercy on me," begged the man. "I'm not really a thief. I came to help my wife, who is expecting our first child. She told me she would die if she didn't have some of your Rapunzel to eat."

Then the witch changed her tune. "By all means," she said, "take as much as you like. But in exchange you must give me the baby when it is born. Don't worry – I will care for it as if I were its mother. What do you say?" The man was so terrified that he hastily agreed to what the witch had said. When his wife gave birth to a baby girl the witch immediately appeared to take the child. The witch named her Rapunzel, after the plants that had caused all the trouble, and took the child away with her.

Rapunzel grew very beautiful, strong and healthy, with long golden hair that fell past her waist. When she was twelve years old the witch locked her away at the top of a tower in the middle of a forest. The tower had neither stairs nor a door, but only one window at the top so that nobody but the witch could reach her.

Each day when the witch visited her, she would stand below the girl's window and call out, "Rapunzel, Rapunzel, let down your hair, that I may climb without a stair."

Then the girl would wind her long tresses around the window hook and lower her hair all the way to the ground. The witch would climb up it as if it were a ladder. In this way, Rapunzel's lonely life went on for several years.

One day, a young prince was riding in the forest when he heard a sweet voice. It was Rapunzel singing to herself. The prince was so entranced that he followed the sound and came upon the tower.

But when he could find no way in he became discouraged and rode home. Rapunzel's lovely voice had stirred his heart so deeply, however, that he returned day after day to hear her singing.

One day, as he stood behind a tree, he saw the witch appear and heard her calling, "Rapunzel, Rapunzel, let down your hair, that I may climb without a stair."

Then he saw a mass of golden hair tumble down and watched the witch climb up it to the window. "Is that the way up?" thought the prince. "Then I will climb the golden ladder, too."

The next day, around dusk, the prince went to the tower and called, "Rapunzel, Rapunzel, let down your hair, that I may climb without a stair."

Immediately the tresses fell down and the prince climbed up. At first sight of the prince, Rapunzel was afraid, but the prince addressed her in such a friendly way that she knew she could trust him. "Once I had heard your voice," said the prince, "I couldn't rest until I saw you. Now I cannot rest until you agree to marry me."

Rapunzel by now had fallen truly in love with the young man, so she willingly accepted. "I wish I could come away with you," said Rapunzel. "You must bring some silk with you each time you visit, and I shall weave a ladder of silk and then I will be able to escape."

Each day the witch visited Rapunzel and each night the prince came. The witch suspected nothing until one day Rapunzel forgot herself and said to the witch, "Why are you so much heavier to pull up than the prince?"

"Oh, treacherous girl," screamed the witch. "You have deceived me!" She snatched up a pair of scissors and cut off all Rapunzel's lovely hair. Then the witch drove Rapunzel from the tower and left her in a wild and desolate place to fend for herself as best she could.

That night, along came the prince to the tower and said, as usual, "Rapunzel, Rapunzel, let down your hair, that I may climb without a stair."

But the witch was lying in wait. She tied Rapunzel's hair to the window hook and let the golden tresses fall to the ground. Up climbed the prince full of joy, as always. But when he stepped in through the window, it was not his beautiful Rapunzel that met his gaze but the icy glare of the witch. "Aha!" cried the witch with a sneer. "So you thought you could steal my girl, did you? Well she's gone and you'll never set eyes on her again."

Beside himself with grief, the prince threw himself from the tower and would have died had he not landed in the thickest briars. Although he survived, the thorns pierced his eyes and blinded him. For many years he wandered through the wilderness grieving for his lost Rapunzel and living on whatever he could find to eat. Eventually, he wandered into the same part of the wilderness where Rapunzel lived in miserable poverty with the twins she had borne.

Just as he had done so many years ago, the prince heard a sweet voice coming through the trees. He made his way towards the sound of the voice. Suddenly Rapunzel saw him and straight away she recognised him. She ran to him and threw her arms around him weeping. As she wept tears of joy and sorrow, two teardrops fell into his eyes, healing them and restoring his sight.

Then the two were united again and the prince took Rapunzel and their children back to his own kingdom, and they all lived happily ever after.

Little Red Riding Hood

There was once a little girl who was given a lovely, bright red cloak by her grandmother. The little girl loved this cloak very much. She loved it so much in fact that she never wanted to take it off, and was always wearing it. Because of this, she became known as Little Red Riding Hood.

One sunny morning, Little Red Riding Hood's mother asked her if she would take some cakes and apple juice to her grandmother, who was ill.

Little Red Riding Hood loved her grandmother very much, and was pleased to be going to visit her.

"But don't delay," said Little Red Riding Hood's mother, "go straight to your grandmother's house and don't play in the forest on the way."

Little Red Riding Hood promised to do as she was told, and said goodbye to her mother and set off.

On the way to her grandmother's house, Little Red Riding Hood met a wolf walking through the forest. Now Little Red Riding Hood did not know that he was wicked, and so she said, "Good morning, Mr Wolf."

"Well, good morning, Little Red Riding Hood," replied the wolf, "and where are you going?"

"I am going to visit my grandmother, who is ill in bed," said Little Red Riding Hood.

"What have you got in your basket, Little Red Riding Hood?" asked the wolf.

"I've got some cakes and a jug of apple juice," said Little Red Riding Hood.

"And where does your grandmother live?" asked the wolf.

"She lives in the forest, not far from here," said Little Red Riding Hood. "Her house is easy to find. It's right next to the lake."

Now the reason that the wolf was asking all these questions was because he really wanted to gobble up Little Red Riding Hood and her grandmother. Suddenly he thought of a cunning plan. "Little Red Riding Hood," he said, "I have an idea! Why don't you pick some of those beautiful flowers which are growing in the forest and give them to your sick grandmother?"

"What a good idea," said Little Red Riding Hood. "My grandmother would be so pleased to have some of these pretty flowers. I'm sure they would make her feel better."

And with that, she set about picking a big bunch of the prettiest flowers she could find. In fact, she was so busy looking for flowers that she didn't see the crafty wolf skip away and make off towards her grandmother's house. The wolf soon came to the house, and knocked on the door.

"Who is it?" said Grandmother.

"It's me, Little Red Riding Hood," said the wolf. "I've brought you some cakes and a jug of apple juice."

"Come in, come in, my dear," said Grandmother, "the door isn't locked."

The wolf then went into the house, and as soon as he saw the old lady lying in bed, he ran straight over to her and gobbled her up. Next he put on her nightgown and her frilly night cap and jumped into her bed, pulling the comforter up to his chin.

In a little while, Little Red Riding Hood – who had by now picked a lovely bunch of flowers for her grandmother – came hurrying up the garden path. The door to her grandmother's house was still open and so she went inside and walked over to the bed. Little Red Riding Hood could only see a little bit of her face poking out from the comforter.

"My, Grandmother, what big ears you have," said Little Red Riding Hood.

"All the better to hear you with, my dear," said the wolf.

"My, Grandmother, what big eyes you have," said Little Red Riding Hood.

"All the better to see you with, my dear," said the wolf.

"My, Grandmother, what big hands you have," said Little Red Riding Hood.

"All the better to hold you tight with, my dear," said the wolf.

"My, Grandmother, what big teeth you have," said Little Red Riding Hood.

"All the better to eat you with, my dear," cried the wolf. And with that he jumped out of bed and gobbled her up.

The wolf felt very full and rather sleepy after he had eaten Little Red Riding Hood. After all, he'd already just eaten her grandmother, too. So he went back to bed and fell asleep, snoring loudly.

Just then, a hunter was passing the house and heard the snoring. He looked through the window, and when he saw the wolf lying in bed, he realized that the wolf must have eaten the old lady. So, while the wolf was still sleeping, the hunter took his knife and cut open the wolf's stomach. To the hunter's great surprise, out popped Little Red Riding Hood and her grandmother. Luckily, the hunter had arrived just in time and both were still alive.

Little Red Riding Hood and her grandmother both thanked the hunter for saving them, and the hunter took the dead wolf's skin and went home.

Little Red Riding Hood's grandmother ate the cakes and drank the apple juice, and soon she was feeling much better. And Little Red Riding Hood? Well, she decided that she would never talk to a wolf again!

BIRTHDAY BUNNIES

"It's my first birthday tomorrow!" announced Snowy, a little white rabbit, very proudly. "Isn't that exciting?"

"Yes, very exciting!" said Whiskers, her brother. "Because it's my birthday too!"

"And mine!" said Patch.

"And mine!" said Nibble.

"And mine!" said Twitch.

"Do you think mom and dad have got a surprise for us?" asked Snowy.

"I hope so!" said Whiskers.

"Me too!" said Patch.

"Me too!" said Nibble.

"Me too!" said Twitch.

Mrs Rabbit was listening outside the door, as her children were getting ready for bed. She heard the little bunnies chattering excitedly about their birthdays the next day.

Whatever could she do to make it a special day for them? She sat and thought very hard, and later that evening, when Mr Rabbit came home, she said: "It is the childrens' first birthday tomorrow, and I'm planning a surprise for them. I want to make them a carrot cake, but I will need some carrots. Could you go and dig some nice fresh ones up from your vegetable garden?"

"Certainly, dear," said Mr Rabbit, and off he went back outside.

Mr Rabbit was proud of the carrots he grew. They were very fine carrots, crunchy and sweet and delicious. Every year he entered them in the Country Show, and they nearly always won first prize. So you can imagine his dismay when he arrived at his vegetable patch to find that every single carrot had been dug up and stolen!

He marched back inside. "Someone has stolen my carrots!" he announced to his wife, crossly. "And I am going to find out just who it is!"

And although it was getting late, he went back outside, and set off to find the naughty person.

First of all he stopped at Hungry Hare's house, and knocked at the door.

"Someone has stolen my carrots!" Mr Rabbit said. "Do you know who?"

"Oh, yes," said Hungry Hare. "But it wasn't me." And although Mr Rabbit pressed him, Hungry Hare would say no more.

Next Mr Rabbit went to Sly Fox's house.

"Someone has stolen my carrots!" he said. "Do you know who?"

"Oh, yes," said Sly Fox. "But it wasn't me." And although Mr Rabbit begged and pleaded with him, Sly Fox would say no more.

So Mr Rabbit marched to Bill Badger's house, and asked if he knew who had taken the carrots.

"Why, yes, in fact I do," said Bill Badger. "But it wasn't me."

And just like the others, he would say no more. It was the same wherever Mr Rabbit went, and although he got very cross, and stamped his foot, no one would tell him who had stolen his carrots!

"You'll find out soon enough," said Red Squirrel.

So Mr Rabbit went home feeling very puzzled.

"It seems that everyone knows who it was, but no one will tell me!" said Mr Rabbit to his wife.

"Not everyone, dear," she said. "I don't know who it was either. All I know is that it's our childrens' first birthday tomorrow, and we have no surprise for them." And feeling very miserable and confused, they went to bed, determined to get to the bottom of the mystery in the morning.

Next day the little bunnies came running into the kitchen, where their parents were having breakfast.

"Happy birthday, everyone!" called Snowy.

"Happy birthday!" cried the other little bunnies.

"Now, it's not much, but I wanted to give each of you a surprise!" Snowy went on. "By the way, I hope you don't mind, Dad." And with that Snowy pulled out a box of juicy carrots, each tied with a bow, and handed one to each of her brothers and sisters.

"Snap!" cried Whiskers, "I had just the same idea!" and he pulled out another box of carrots.

"Me too!" said Patch.

"Me too!" said Nibble.

"Me too!" said Twitch.

Soon there was a great pile of juicy carrots heaped on the kitchen table.

"So that's what happened to my carrots!" cried Mr Rabbit, in amazement. "I thought they had been stolen! And when he told the little bunnies the story they laughed till their sides ached. Then Mrs Rabbit put on her apron and shooed them outside.

"Just leave the carrots with me," she said. "I have a birthday surprise of my own in store!"

And so the mystery was solved. It turned out that Hungry Hare had seen the little bunnies creep out one by one, and each dig up a few carrots when they thought no one was looking. He knew it was their birthdays and he guessed what they were doing. He had told the other forest folk, and everyone thought it was a great joke.

Mr Rabbit felt very ashamed that he had been so cross with everyone, when they were really just keeping the secret. To apologise, he invited them for a special birthday tea that afternoon, which the little bunnies thought was a great surprise.

And of course the highlight of the day was when Mrs Rabbit appeared from the kitchen carrying, what else, but an enormous carrot cake!

BARNEY THE BOASTFUL BEAR

Barney was a very boastful bear.

"Look at my lovely soft fur!" he would say to the other toys. "See how it shines!"

Barney loved to talk about himself. "I'm the smartest toy in the playroom!" he would say. "It's a well-known fact."

He didn't know that the other toys all laughed about him behind his back.

"That bear thinks he's so smart," growled Scotty Dog. "But he isn't smart enough to know when everyone's fed up with him!"

"He'll learn his lesson one of these days," said Molly Monkey, and sure enough, that is just what happened...

One hot summer's day, the toys lazed in the warm playroom. "Wouldn't it be lovely if we could go for a walk outside," said Rag Doll.

"We could have a lovely picnic in the woods!" said Old Bear.

"Even better, we could go for a drive in the toy car first!" said Rabbit.

"But none of us is big or clever enough to drive the toy car," said Rag Doll, sadly.

"I am!" came a voice from the corner. It was Barney. He had been listening to them talking.

"I can drive the toy car. And I know the best place for a picnic in the woods," he said.

"We've never seen you drive the car," said Rabbit, suspiciously.

"That's because I drive it at night, when you're asleep," said Barney. "I'm a very good driver, in fact."

"Ooh, let's go then!" cried Rag Doll. And in no time they had packed up a picnic and were sitting ready in the car.

"Er, I don't feel like driving today, actually," mumbled Barney. "It's too hot." But the others

were not interested in hearing excuses, so rather reluctantly Barney climbed into the driver's seat and started the engine. You see, the truth was, Barney had never really driven the car before, and he was scared. But he wanted to show off, so he pretended to know what he was doing.

Off they set down the garden path. "Toot, toot!" Barney beeped the horn as he turned the little car out into the country lane, and soon they were driving along, singing merrily.

All was going well, until Rag Doll suddenly said, "Hey, Barney, didn't we just miss the turning for the woods?"

"I know where I'm going," said Barney, crossly. "Leave it to me." And he made the little car go faster.

"Slow down a bit, Barney!" called Old Bear, from the back seat. "My fur is getting all ruffled." He was starting to feel anxious.

"I don't need a back seat driver, thank you," said Barney, with a growl, and made the car go even faster. By now the others were starting to feel scared, but Barney was having a great time.

"Aren't I a wonderful driver!" he chuckled. "Look – no hands!" And he took his paws off the steering wheel. Just then they reached a sharp corner. The little car went spinning off the side of the road and crashed into a tree, tipping all the toys out into the ditch!

They were a bit dazed, but luckily no one was hurt. They were not pleased with Barney though.

"You silly bear!" said Rabbit, crossly. "We could have all been badly hurt!"

"We'll have to walk home now," said Rag Doll, rubbing her head. "Where are we?"

Everyone looked at Barney.

"Don't ask me!" he said, quietly.

"But you said you knew the way!" said Old Bear, indignantly.

"I was only pretending," said Barney, his voice trembling. "I don't really know how to drive, and I don't know where we are!" And he started to cry.

The other toys were furious with Barney.

"You naughty boastful bear!" they scolded. "Now see what trouble your boasting has got us into!"

The lost toys walked through the dark woods all night long, clinging together in fright as shadows loomed around them.

They had never been out at night before. Then just before dawn, they spotted the little house where they lived, and crept back into the playroom.

What a relief it was to be home again!

Luckily their owner had not noticed they were missing, so she never knew what an adventure her toys had been having while she was fast asleep. She often wondered what had happened to her toy car though.

As for Barney, he was very sorry for the trouble he had caused. After a while the other toys forgave him, and from that day on he never boasted about anything again.

LITTLE SHEEP

Little Sheep couldn't sleep,
Not a wink, not a peep!
Tossing, turning, all night through,
What was poor Little Sheep to do?

Owl came by, old and wise,
Said, "Silly sheep, use your eyes –
You're lying in a field of sheep,
Try counting them to help you sleep!"

"Seven, four, thirteen, ten –
That's not right, I'll start again..."
Till daylight came, awake he lay
And vowed he'd learn to count next day!

GIRAFFE'S SONG

It's wonderful having a long neck,
That reaches right up to the sky,
You can nibble the leaves on the treetops,
And smile at the birds flying by.

It's wonderful having a long neck,
You can see for miles around,
You always know just where
your friends are,
And where the best food can be found.

It's wonderful having a long neck,
Although, I'm not meaning to gloat.
For there's one time that I really curse it,
And that's when I get a sore throat!